Six Feet Down

By Bob Moats

This book is a novella, shorter than a novel, but longer than a short story.

Table of Contents

For information and address:
Magic 1 Productions
P.O. Box 524, Fraser MI 48026-0524
Website: http://murdernovels.com

Cover design by Bob Moats
Stock photo www.fotosearch.com

SYNOPSIS: Jake Wyler bought a cemetery. It was one of those impulse buys and now he was having to spend a large portions of his life savings to be a property owner. He had returned to his hometown to find his life turned upside down and involved in murder, missing money and love letters. He meets an old high school classmate and she handles his money in the bank where she works. Jake has no idea how to run a cemetery and since the former owner was murdered, he was now really lost. It seems Jake gave the former owner the purchase money in cash and someone murdered him for the money, hidden in the house on the cemetery property. Jake and the son of his lady banker turn the house over to find the hidden cash and come up with nothing. Two times the house had been broken into and was almost was cause for Jake's own murder. A new book about an ordinary guy caught in mysteries and dead bodies. This book is a novella.

Extra special thanks to:

To Susan Haughton, for editing my chapters.

TO THE PROOF READERS, Amy Morningstar, Cindy Valstad, Carolyn Linington and Al Norris for proofing the final copy and hopefully catching all those annoying little errors that slip through.

TO RUSS HOLTHAUS, A police officer, who made sure my characters didn't violate any laws.

THANK YOU TO ALL THE people who purchased this book. I hope you enjoy it as much as I enjoyed writing it for my faithful readers.

THE BOB MOATS FAMILY of Readers is listed in the back of the book.

Chapter 1

I was a government employee for the National Archives for the last 30 years. I catalogued artifacts and documents left behind by our forefathers and documented the history of the United States of America. I finally became disillusioned by the lies that I saw from the stories between the men who started this country all the way through to the present century. I had to get out since I started to learn what price we paid for our indiscretions. I quit and went out into the private sector. That's how I ended up buying a cemetery.

Washington, D.C. was getting on my nerves so I moved back to my childhood town of Fraser, Michigan, and found a small, cheap apartment. Ever since I started working in D.C. I had saved a portion of my pay in a savings account and after 30 years I had enough to get by for quite a while. I was in my sixties and didn't want to sit around, so I needed a job to keep busy. I finally found a part time job in a local library. I was known in the city since I grew up there and the people at the library all knew me.

My home town has two cemeteries within the city, one owned by the local Catholic Church and one privately owned. I had passed the privately owned one a number of times after I got back home. One afternoon as I drove along the main road out of town to go shopping for groceries, I saw a sign out front of the privately owned cemetery that said it was for sale. I was amazed that a cemetery could be sold, but there was the sign.

I pulled over and wrote down the phone number that was crudely written on the bottom of the sign, probably purchased at the local dollar store. I pulled out my cell phone and dialed the number. I don't know why the thought of buying a cemetery intrigued me. As a teen I used to play in that cemetery at night with a couple buddies I had. We'd crouch behind the tombstones and play hide and seek, usually scaring the crap out of the person trying to find us. My first kiss was in this cemetery. Lana Crawford and I braved the place to park and nature took its course. So I had a history with that hallowed piece of land.

The phone rang and was answered, "Yeah, Whatcha want?" a man said in a gruff voice. I immediately recognized it as old man Crenshaw, the man who owned the property. He had chased us out of the place on a number of occasions.

"Mr. Crenshaw, my name is Jake Wyler and I'm calling about your for sale sign."

"You wanna buy the sign?" he growled.

"No, sir, the property."

"Say, are you Dick Wyler's kid?"

"I'm hardly a kid now and yes, my father was Dick Wyler."

"What's the old bastard doing now?"

"Sorry, the old bastard passed away eight years ago. As a matter of fact, he's buried in your cemetery."

"Damn, that's too bad that he kicked the bucket. I use to drink with him at the VFW until we couldn't stand."

"Yes, and then he'd come home and beat on me. I don't regret his passing."

"Oh, I didn't know that, sorry. Well, you interested in the property?"

"I may be, if the price is right. I don't suppose it makes any money?"

"Hell, no. The stiffs pay once then they take up space. I was going to dig them all up and move them but the city told me I couldn't. The upkeep is getting too much for me. Cutting grass and weeding is not what I want to do for the rest of my life. Trying to find people to do the job is not easy either, they want to be paid."

"I'm at the cemetery now, can we meet?"

"You should know I live next to the cemetery, since I had to chase you and those other brats out. I'll be there shortly." He hung up and I backed the car to the dirt drive that wound around the place. I stopped at the place where Lana and I parked and was startled when he knocked on my window.

"Geez, you got old," he said as I got out.

"Well, you don't look so hot yourself," I replied. He did look like he was a candidate for burial in the place.

He laughed and said, "We all grow too old too soon. Now do you want the cemetery?"

I looked around and asked, "Have you had many people asking about it?"

"Hell, no. Who wants to own a cemetery? You're the first to ask."

I moved to an area that I was told where they buried my old man. I found the simple flat headstone that the Veteran's Administration bought for him. He was once a career soldier in the Marines, but he took a bullet to his leg and couldn't get around without a limp.

Crenshaw stood next to me and said, "May he rest in peace."

I thought he could rest in hell for all he put me through. When I was eighteen I joined the Marines, which made him proud. I only joined to get away from him. I grew up in the Marines, seeing lots of combat during the couple wars that the U.S. had stuck their noses in, and then they put me in a special ops section. I lasted there about ten years before I got out and went to work in D.C.

I turned away from the headstone and went back to my car. "How much do you want for it?"

"I want to get out of this damn town so I'm making you a real good deal. 250K and it's yours.

"Will you stay long enough to get me started? I've never owned a cemetery before."

"I'll stay for a short time, then I'm gone. You want the place?"

"Does your house come with it?"

"It's on cemetery property, so it does. It needs lots of work to clean it up. I'm not a damn housekeeper."

I mulled it over. I knew I had the money in my savings, but I would have to scrimp after dropping 250k. I looked around; the place had a nice feel to it, despite the headstones standing tall. I guess my love of things past, things forgotten, made me say, "I'll take it."

Chapter 2

"You just bought yourself a cemetery," he said as he held out his hand for me to shake. Most of these older men in this small town used a handshake like a contract. I reached out and shook.

"I'll have to go to the bank in the morning and get a certified check," I said.

"Oh, hell, no," he said the words slowly, stretched out. "I don't put any faith in banks, least of all in this town. I'll need cash."

"Crenshaw…Ben, I don't know if the bank would have that much on hand. It may take a day for them to get that much in."

"Well, we'll wait, then. No checks or money orders. I want cold, hard, cash."

"Okay, I'm not agreeable to handling that much money, but if you insist. What are you going to do with it when I bring it to you?"

"That's my business and no one else's. Just have the cash and the deal is done."

I was a little worried. I just put all my money in one of the banks in town, I wondered what they would say. Not that I cared, it was my money.

"Okay, I'll go stop by my bank and let them start the procedure, then I'll see you in the morning, hopefully with the cash." I thought it was crazy, but it's what he wanted.

"I'll call you when I find out what happens." I got into my car and drove out, leaving him standing amongst the tombstones.

I gave up on getting groceries, I still had food, so I drove to my bank. I went in and over to a woman seated in a cubicle. I recognized her from high school, Becky Trudell, she looked good for her age. I was in my sixties so she had to be also. I stood at the opening to her cubicle and waited for her to notice me.

She finally looked over and said, "May I help you?"

I waited to see if she recognized me, but she sat staring. "Becky, it's me, Jake Wyler."

She squinted her eyes and I realized she needed her glasses. She reached down and picked up a pair of them from her desk and put them on. Now I could see the recognition.

"Oh, my god. It is you, Jake. How are you?"

"I'm good, how are you doing?"

"Well, after graduation, I just floated from job to job, then about twenty years ago, I ended up pregnant by Eddie Grabowski and the bastard skipped out. I had to go on welfare, thank goodness for that. I had a baby boy and we moved in with my parents. I got a job as a teller here and then they finally moved me up to being an assistant manager. Other than that I'm doing well. You?"

I didn't really want to get into my life, so I said, "I did good, joined the Marines and after that I worked in Washington D.C. in the National Archives. Now I'm back here and need help with my account."

"Oh, yes, business as usual. Have a seat and tell me what you need."

I sat next to her desk and said, "I need two hundred and fifty thousand dollars from my account, in cash."

She just stared some more and said, "We don't have that much in the bank that can be handed out all at once."

"Well, that's why I'm here now. I'll need it in the morning. I'm buying the old cemetery on Main Street, north of town."

Now her eyes went wide, "You're buying that cemetery?"

"Yes, is there a problem?"

"You've been gone a long time, right? So you don't know about all the talk regarding the cemetery."

"Yes, I've been gone over forty years, so I'm a little out of the loop. What's wrong with the cemetery?"

"The gossip is that the cemetery is haunted. There have been strange lights and sounds coming from the property. Old man Crenshaw won't even go in there at night. Or so the police have reported."

"I hope there are no ghosts in there. I don't want to buy the place if it's haunted."

"Well, that's up to you. Now I have to start a request for your funds. Do you have your account number?"

I took a slip of paper from my wallet and read the numbers to her. She typed the numbers into her computer and then studied it.

"Wow, you do have some money, don't you?" she exclaimed.

"It's been thirty years of savings. It did add up, didn't it?"

"I'll say. So you need two hundred and fifty K? I think we can handle that. I'll call Corporate and have them start the transfer. A truck should be here in the morning. Do you have a bag to put it in?"

"I can get one, how big of a bag?"

"A large gym bag will do."

"I have one of those, thanks."

"That's all I need for now. Anything else I can help you with?"

"No, I'm good. I do have one question, when I opened my account was there any gift to be given?"

"Yes, a fondue pot. Didn't you get one?"

"No, that's why I'm asking. You don't have a toaster?"

"You don't like fondue?"

"Not really, cheese makes me gaseous," I said with a smile. I didn't have any problem with cheese, I loved cheese but I didn't want a fondue pot.

"Let me look in our storage area and see what we have." She said and stood. She had a nice figure, surprising for her age. I don't want to be sexist, but women when they get older they develop a few extra pounds in the wrong places. Becky looked good. Great, now I am being sexist. I put my mind on the cemetery and the hauntings. I hoped they were just silly rumors, but I would have to pin down Crenshaw about it.

Becky came back and was holding a box with a toaster. "I found this in the back from an older promotion. It's yours, and thank you for your business."

I took it and smiled, thinking about asking her for a drink later. Now, is that sexist?

Chapter 3

I gave up on the idea about a drink when I saw the diamond rings on her married finger. I guess all the good women are taken. I thanked her and left the bank. I put the toaster on the passenger seat. I needed one since mine had died. I drove out and went to my apartment, since I didn't feel like going back to the cemetery, I'd have plenty of time for that.

I entered my apartment and put the toaster on the kitchen counter. I cut open the box and took out the toaster, putting it on the counter where the old one was. I had thrown it out a few days ago, this new one was a welcome sight.

It was now after five in the afternoon and I was missing my nap time. I never took a nap until the last couple years. I would get back up by seven and then watch TV until eight when I would open that first beer of the evening. I needed to go relieve my bladder and as I was in the bathroom, I looked at myself in the mirror. I looked like a recluse, which I was becoming. I had a beard but the area around that was in need of shaving and the beard needed trimming. The hair on my head was in need of combing and a good grooming. I was determined to go get a haircut since I was going to be a landowner now.

That was all I needed to see for now. I went in to grab a quick hour long nap and then to spend the night being catatonic in front of the TV. I watched up until the news, then shut it off. I didn't like watching the news, it was too depressing. And this comes from a guy who is going to own a cemetery.

I slept well that night, no bad dreams about bodies rising up out of graves. I dressed and shaved, trimming my beard and combing my hair. I looked somewhat presentable now.

I waited until the bank opened and gave it a little extra time for the money truck to arrive. I made toast with the new toaster and it worked great, just right. I cleaned up the mess on the kitchen counter and went out to the car. I drove to the bank and saw the armored truck just pulling away. My money was here. I took the empty gym bag in and went to Becky's cubicle. She smiled at me, with her glasses on, and took me to a teller. She explained the situation and they brought my money out.

I was amazed by how much 250k piled up. I started to put the money in my bag and it fit well. I zipped up the bag as Becky said, "Be careful, that's a lot of money."

"I know, but Crenshaw insisted on cash."

"Do you know the man is crazy?"

"No, I don't. How crazy?"

"It's a long story, maybe I could tell you his history over drinks some night."

That caught me off guard. "I thought by your rings, that you were married."

"No, these are costume jewelry; I wear them to keep creeps from hitting on me."

"What makes you think I'm not a creep?"

"I don't know, you just seem different. We can discuss this later."

"Okay, after I become the proud owner of a cemetery, I'll call you to go for a drink and maybe dinner."

"Throw in a movie and I'm sold."

I smiled and said I'd be in touch. I had to get the money to Crenshaw.

I left the bank with a pleasant memory of Becky standing, watching me leave. I threw the bag into my car and drove back to the cemetery. I called Crenshaw to let him know I had the money. He seemed pleased.

I pulled into the dirt drive and over to the house, and saw Crenshaw standing at the front of the house. I pulled up, took the bag out and handed it to him.

"I won't count it, I trust you," he said and then went into his house, leaving me on the sidewalk. He came out a few minutes later and I wondered what he did with the money. He handed my empty bag back and smiled.

"Here's the quit claim deed," he said, handing a piece of paper to me. I opened it and could see it was official. "Take it to the county register of deeds, file it and the property is yours. Pleasure doing business with you. I'll clear out my personal property from the house this week and you can take over."

"I hope you'll stay long enough to guide me through the routine of working a cemetery."

"Not much, just agree to bury someone, dig a hole six feet down and let the people come and drop their loved one in. Then, when they leave, cover the hole back up and you're done. Simple enough, and don't forget to take their money."

I thought it sounded simple, like a storage facility, but more permanent. "Okay, I'm going to the county building and file the deed. I'll be back to take a look inside the house."

"Don't expect a palace. I haven't done much with it in years. You'll have lot of work to do. Or you could burn it down and build a new house. I'll explain the bills you'll have to take care of and how to deal with funeral directors. They are an ornery bunch. There are a couple of them in town who are easy to deal with. I'll let you in on how to work with them."

"Thanks, I'll be back." I went to my car and drove up to the county building to file the deed. I had to stand in line for about an hour and then they took the quit claim and filed it.

I was now the proud owner of property that held hundreds of dead bodies. I wondered if that was something good, or a bit morbid.

Chapter 4

I didn't have to work at the library today, only on Mondays, Wednesdays and Fridays. I figured after I got into the swing of things at the cemetery, I'd either quit the library or cut back on days. All I did was put books back on the shelves and repair damaged books. Sort of like I did at the Archive.

I headed back to the house that Crenshaw was still occupying and drove up the dirt road to the place. I stood at my car looking over to the cemetery just across the road from the house and saw the grass needed cutting as badly as the hair on my head.

I heard a noise behind me and turned to see Crenshaw coming out of the house. He came down the short set of steps and over to me.

"Ready for the grand tour of your new dwelling?" he said, looking too happy. I guess he would be, getting away from this all. I hoped I didn't end up like him living in a cemetery. I was now wondering why I did this.

I had only seen the house from the road, but now as we approached, I could see the sad condition it was in. The paint on the wood siding was peeling and cracking. The windows looked like they hadn't been cleaned in years. I wondered how he could see out. The porch creaked under our weight and I knew it was only a matter of time before I'd go through it. There were shutters on the front windows but two of the shutters hung crookedly by one nail. I wondered if it wasn't a bad idea to burn it down and start over.

We entered. "I said it wasn't a palace. I'm not handy at fixing things, I hope you are," he said, as he led the way like a real estate agent trying to sell this house.

We left the vestibule that was actually very Victorian, probably when the house was built. I figured with a good cleaning, the stained glass and the parquet flooring would stand up well. We entered a living room that had very little furniture, which surprised me. There was a couch, chair, coffee table and a television on milk cartons. On the outer wall was a large fireplace that he probably burned his other furniture in. I couldn't see him cutting trees down and chopping them into firewood.

"I don't have lots to take, so you can keep the furniture. The TV only gets five channels, I never put in an outside antenna. I'll show you the kitchen," he said as we went through an arched opening to a hallway. We came into the kitchen and it looked like it had seen many meals served. I was surprised by the wood stove. Now I knew what he had done with the rest of the furniture.

"I use a microwave for my meals, mostly TV dinners I get at the Dollar Tree. Banquet makes pretty good meals." He pointed to the microwave on the counter.

"I buy most of my groceries and things from the Dollar Tree," I said now knowing with the money I paid him, I would be shopping more at the Dollar Tree. "How do you heat in the winter?"

"There's a fuel oil furnace in the back and the tank is outside away from the house. I got past building codes by grandfathering it in. Damn government wants to tell us how to live. Of course, since you are the new owner, they probably will force you to upgrade to gas. Just don't tell them you are the new owner."

He took me out to a stairway that was very ornate, showing the craftsmanship they did in years back. We went up and to a bedroom, which had a bed, dresser and a chair. Ben Crenshaw liked to live a Spartan life. I noticed the drawers on the dresser were all open and empty, and then I saw the steamer trunk full of clothes. He was already starting to pack.

"The other bedroom is empty, I never had any use for it. The bathroom is down here." He led me out the door and down the hallway. He opened that door and we stepped inside. It was an old bathroom with old fixtures. It actually had a tub with feet. I hadn't seen one of those in years.

"I don't bathe but once a month so the tub is clean. The toilet works but you have to hold the handle down until you hear it gurgle, then let up. I probably should have fixed it, but I'm going nowhere fast, anyway."

He walked out and I followed him back down the stairs. There was one more room he took me to, his office. He went to the desk that was covered in papers and said, "You have bills, of course. Electricity, fuel oil, water bills, and the property tax, which only comes twice a year. It's big so save some money."

"Just how big is the property?"

"About six acres, more than half is filled with dead people, still plenty of room for more. If you play your cards right, you can get to be friends with the funeral people and steer business here."

I didn't realize that I would have to suck up to them for dead people. I guess it could be worse. I knew this wouldn't be a money making venture, I just wanted to have a place to take care of. This place was in need of taking care of, for sure.

"I think I'd like to go wander amongst the graves, just to familiarize myself with the lay of the land." I started towards the door, stopped and turned. "Where do you keep the lawn equipment and weed wacker?" I asked.

"There's a shed just down this road and everything is in there. I've been lucky that nothing has been stolen out of it since I've been here."

"Thanks," I said and left. I walked across the road to the edge of the cemetery proper and entered. I felt strange, like I walked into a fairy land. I hoped it wasn't ghosts surrounding me. I checked out the headstones towards the front of the property, then I saw the for sale sign and went down the slight hill and pulled it up.

I set it down at the top of the hill and went back to reading the headstones. I was amazed by the years on the stones. Most in the front were from the early 1800s and the names were from families that I knew in town.

I explored a while longer then felt a hunger pang, so I went back to my car and since I didn't see Crenshaw, I just drove out.

Chapter 5

I went back to my apartment and made a baloney and cheese sandwich. I sat eating and thinking about what I had just done. I spent more than half of my savings on a cemetery that I had no idea how to run. But how difficult could it be? As Crenshaw said, agree to bury a body, dig six feet down, drop the person in and cover. I was only concerned about digging the six foot hole. I was not very active in doing manual labor, but I had enough money left to hire a front scoop operator. I was sure Crenshaw didn't dig the graves.

I finished my sandwich and decided to go to the library to talk to Margaret, the head librarian, and explain my plight of cutting my days back. I went to my car and drove over. I entered through the employee entrance and found Margaret at her desk. She smiled as I approached and said, "What are you doing here on your day off?"

"I have a situation that I need to work out about changing my days."

"Talk to me," she said.

I explained that I bought the old Crenshaw cemetery and I felt I may be a bit busy with it for a while. It needed work to clean it up.

"You're right. I always thought that the place was running down from what I could see driving by. You'll have a lot of work ahead of you," she said.

As we spoke, more of the women who worked there were gathering when they could hear what was being said.

Julie said, "You bought that cemetery? I didn't know they could sell a cemetery."

I looked up at her and said, "If the price is right you can buy one. I had to dip into my savings, but I had enough."

Another girl, Tammy, asked, "How much did it cost?"

Margaret spoke up, "Tammy, that's not something you should ask."

I smiled and said it was all right. "It was a lot of money, but I had it. Crenshaw is going to be well off now, and I'll be getting by."

Julie said, "I heard he socks his money away under his bed, he doesn't trust banks."

"Well, that may be true, I had to pay him in cash. I don't know what he did with it. Maybe put it in one of the graves," I joked.

They all laughed and the girls went off. I said to Margaret, "I'll let you know how it goes after I take over. I only took this job here so I wouldn't be bored at home. Owning a cemetery will not be boring."

She agreed. I stood and said, "I'll still be here on my next day until you can find a replacement."

"I wouldn't worry about that. There are tons of students who need a part time job. So call and let me know what is happening. Are you going to give burial discounts to friends?" she said with a big grin.

I laughed and said, "We'll see. Thanks for the job, Margaret, I'll be in touch." I went out and to my car. I drove back to the cemetery and found the shed Ben had talked about. It had a lock on it but it wasn't closed and the key was in it. I presume Ben had left it open for me, so I took out the key and put it in my pocket.

I opened the door and looked in. There was a light switch that I turned on and saw the lawnmower and a weedwacker. It was a gas powered wacker which made it easy to use. The lawnmower looked fairly new, not much crud built up on it. Crenshaw probably didn't use it much.

I wasn't going to do any trimming today, but I could start bright and early tomorrow. I closed up the shed and went to my car. I didn't see the old man, so I presumed he was watching TV or something. I had a few more questions for him, but they could wait. I got in my car and drove around and back to the entrance and out.

My cell phone buzzed and I pulled over. I answered even though it said it was a private number. "Hello?"

"Jake, this is Becky from the bank. Did you get the money to Ben Crenshaw?"

"I did and I have no idea what he did with it. But that's his problem now. I filed the deed and the cemetery is all mine. I really am thinking I'm crazy but I kind of like the idea. Now I have lots of work to do to bring the place into ship shape condition. I really could use some help, but I'll give it time before I get too overworked."

"If you need some cheap labor, my son is looking for work. He been out of high school for a while and he could use some manual labor."

"Well, that would be great. If he can manage a lawnmower, he's hired. Give me a day to get organized and I'll call you. Oh, I'll need your number, it came up private on my phone."

She gave me the number and I wrote it on the paper note pad I carried in my car. "Good, I'll let you know soon. Oh, if you still are open for a drink, dinner and a movie, we can discuss that, too."

I heard her laugh, it was pleasant and soft. "I'll be looking forward to it. I'll wait for your call about my son, thanks, and talk to you later." She hung up and I put my phone back in my pocket.

I glanced at my watch and it was getting close to my nap time so I headed back to the apartment. I made a quick bowl of soup for dinner and then went to lay down.

I dreamt of graves opening up and people coming out, then I started to run the lawnmower over them and they retreated. I woke in a sweat. "Damn, I hope this is not going to be a regular thing now."

Chapter 6

I needed a diversion after that dream and I felt like calling Becky. It was only just before six so it was still early enough to take her to dinner. I pulled my cell phone out and dialed the number she gave me. After two rings, she answered.

"Becky, it's Jake, I hope I didn't interrupt something important?" I said.

"No, I was just wondering what I wanted to eat. What's up?"

"That's perfect. How would you like dinner and drinks on me? I just want to get out and celebrate my owning a cemetery. Not very glamorous, but I've never owned one before."

She laughed and said that would be fine with her. "Where are you taking me? It's a little late for a movie."

"If the dinner goes well, we can talk about a movie later."

"So, you want to test me on this date to see if there's going to be a second date?"

Now I laughed. "It's not going to be a date, just two old friends sharing a dinner."

"I suppose I'll have to pay for my own food."

"No, I'll pay. Since you already know how much is in my bank account, I'm hardly broke. Where do I pick you up at?"

She gave me an address and I said, "Great, I'll pick you up in an hour. I need time to make myself look pretty."

We hung up and I went to take a shower, shave and make myself look pretty. Which wasn't easy. I wasn't bad looking, better than most men. Not exactly Tom Selleck, more like Bruce Willis in his later years. I got dressed in a nice suit and headed out the door. I knew the area she lived in, I just needed to find the house.

I found it and went to the door. I knocked and it was opened by a rather tall, muscular young man. "Hi, does Becky Trudell live here?"

He looked back and yelled, "Mom, your friend is here." He turned back to me and asked, "Are you the guy with the cemetery?"

"I am. Your mother told you about me?"

"She did and she said you might need help in the cemetery with lawn care?"

"I may, would you be interested?"

"I'd think it would be cool to work in a cemetery making it look nice."

Becky came up behind him looking really great in a fairly short, blue dress. "You could have at least invited him in, Paul."

I smiled and said, "I made reservations for 7:30 so we should go. Paul, if you want a job and can be dependable, I'll give you a try. We can both see if it will work out."

"I'd like that, so Mom will get off me about finding a job."

"Paul, you didn't have to say that. Do I bug you about working?"

"Yes," he said and went off from the door. Then yelled from the other room, "I'll expect you to be back at a reasonable hour."

She sighed, "I don't know about kids today. They have minds of their own and we don't have much luck controlling them."

"I don't know, I don't have any children. Shall we go?"

I took her arm and led her to the car. "You never had children, may I ask why?" she said as she got in.

"I never married and sex wasn't a casual thing for me. So no children. I regret it sometimes, but I'm too stuck into being on my own, no ties." I said as I drove to the restaurant.

"Ah, so if I asked you to marry me, I'd be safe?" she said with a smile.

"Yes, you'd have nothing to worry about from me. I've never been the marrying kind. It had to do with my parents. My father was abusive and my mother just accepted it and tried to change him. He drove her to her grave, not killing her, but he was responsible for her death."

"I'm sorry for that. I didn't mean to bring up bad memories."

"No, it just gets things out in the open. Better than talking about it over dinner," I grinned.

She agreed and sat silently as we approached the restaurant. "Well, we are going first class," she said when she saw the place.

"El Charro is a great restaurant and you don't have to order Mexican food, so enjoy yourself." This place was an upscale Mexican restaurant that was highly recommended by many people.

I parked and we went in to find a hostess and she took us to a nice secluded table. The waitress came up and took our drink orders. I asked for a large Pepsi and Becky got a Virgin Mary.

"So, we aren't drinking alcohol?" she said.

"Not when I'm driving. At home I can get potty faced, but never on the road."

"I'm liking you more," she said with a grin.

"Don't get too attached. We can be friends, but nothing more."

"I'm disappointed, but friends are good. So, you met Paul and you think you could use him?"

"He looks healthy enough. I can pay him for his work. It's a big place and lots of grass to cut and headstones to trim, so he will earn his pay."

"Good, he can use it. So, you got the money to Crenshaw safely?"

"Yes, and he took it in his house, now mine, and came out with my bag empty. I don't know what he did with it. He probably has secret panels or removable floor boards to put his money. After he leaves I'll have to find where he hid the money, although there won't be any money in it."

Our drinks came and we sat making small talk about our lives after high school. We ordered dinner, I got a nice sirloin steak dinner and she got lamb chops. We ate in relative silence and finished our meals.

"This is nice, good food and good company," she said wiping her mouth. She had nice lips that I wouldn't mind tasting. "I don't suppose we could go back to your place for real drinks?"

I waved to the waitress and said, "Check, please."

Chapter 7

The ride to my place was brief and quiet. I was afraid to look at her, or she might vanish. I pulled into the parking lot and we went to my apartment. I barely got in the door when she attacked me. I didn't resist.

An hour later, after we wrestled in bed, we lay still. She gave a big sigh. "I haven't been with a man in years. That was the best I can remember."

"Your memory must be faulty."

"Hey, I have a good memory. I also remember that I did have a small crush on you in high school. So this is an accomplishment for me. Fulfilling a dream."

"So, I was just a goal for you?"

She got up on her arm next to me, "No, you aren't. I just have a good feeling about you. Okay, so you're not the marrying type, that's fine. I don't need the aggravation, either, so we have a good thing going." She jumped out of bed and went to the bathroom. I could hear the shower running. I got up and followed her lead. After that, we dried off and dressed.

"Your son said to be home at a reasonable hour. I better take you home or he will be a surly employee for me."

She laughed and kissed me. She tasted good, but I had to resist. We were finished for the night and I had to get her home.

I took her to the car and drove her home. I could see Paul looking out the window. "He worries about you. That's nice," I said.

"He has always mothered me, it's almost annoying. It's only midnight. I won't turn into a pumpkin and I am still his mother." She kissed me again and got out.

"Do you want me to walk you to the door?" I asked.

"No, he'll interrogate you. Best if we say good night here and I'll talk to you tomorrow." She closed the door and went to the house.

I waited until she was in, and then drove away with pleasant memories of the night. It had been years since I had sex with a girl from the Archive. She was a one night stand and I never saw her again. I knew I would see Becky again.

I also knew I didn't want a relationship, so I had to make sure this didn't develop into one. Friends with benefits, they call it. That would work for me.

I went back to my apartment and got into bed. I could still smell her on the pillow and it helped me to sleep.

I woke the next morning feeling energized. The bunny had nothing on me. I showered, dressed and got ready to go start cleaning the cemetery. I went to my car and over to the house. I drove onto the dirt road and was surprised to see two police cars, a CSU SUV and a coroner's van.

I pulled off to the side and parked. I got out and approached the taped off area in front of the house. There was an older cop standing at the tape and he turned to me. "Sir, you can't enter." Then he gave me a good look and said, "Geez, are you Jake Wyler?"

"I am, Scott. Long time no see. I see you became a cop?"

"I did. What are you doing here?"

"Well, I bought this property, this is my house now."

"Are you serious? Old man Crenshaw sold it to you?"

"Yep, what's going on?"

"Someone took out old man Crenshaw. He's dead."

I felt a chill run through my body. Ben Crenshaw was dead and why? "Who's in charge," I asked.

"Mickey France. Remember him? He used to hide with us in this cemetery when we played hide and seek here."

I did remember him. I never fully liked the guy, he was arrogant and a bully. He never bothered me, but he liked to attack the underclass boys.

"He's here?" I asked.

"Sure, come on and I'll take you to him. Since it's now your property, it should be alright."

As we went up the creaking porch, Scott said, "You need to get this fixed before someone hurts themself."

"Hey, this is my first day as property owner and I just came here, only to find a murder, go easy."

He laughed and we went in. Just past the vestibule lay the body of Crenshaw. There was a small pool of blood under him and someone I presumed was the coroner kneeling by him. Two men stood by and one turned to us coming in. I knew right away it was Mickey France, he still had an arrogant look.

"Scott, who's this?" he asked. Then as we got nearer, his face changed. "Damn, is that Jake Wyler?"

Scott said it was and Mickey came to us. "Jake, what are you doing back in town? I thought you got out years ago."

"Yeah, 40 to be exact. I gave up a job with the government in D.C. to come back to this boring little town."

"Boring until we get a murder. It happens now with too much regularity. But it's job security. What are you doing now?"

"Well, for starters, I own this cemetery, bought it yesterday from old man Crenshaw." I looked down at his body, and apologized for calling him old. "What happened?"

"Someone shot him. You own this place now?"

"Yeah, I brought him the money and then filed the deed, so it's mine. I suppose I'll have to bury him here now."

"He had no relatives, they all died off and he was alone. So you're going to have to be responsible for his burial. Seeing as you own a cemetery," he said, with a grin.

"How was he found?" I asked.

"Local funeral director needed to bury a man next to his wife, who's buried here. She tried to get hold of him, but he didn't answer. The woman needed to get the hole dug and put the man in, so she sent one of her assistants out here to find Crenshaw. He got here, found the front door open and came in finding the body. He called us."

"Great, now I have to bury Crenshaw and some guy next to his wife. I don't even know what I'm doing, Crenshaw was supposed to explain all that."

Chapter 8

"Well, you're going to have to learn fast," Mickey said. "After the Crime Scene guys finish and the body is taken, you can have the place, good luck."

The man in the coroner jumpsuit came over and said, "One shot to the heart, it was a good shot or a lucky one. I'll know more when we get him on the slab. Otherwise there's not much to say. Clean kill. He was killed around eight to ten last night."

"Thanks, Doc," Mickey said. The coroner had his men put the body in a bag and on the gurney. They wheeled him out and then I stood looking at the blood stain.

"I can recommend a good crime scene clean up company," Scott said.

"Yeah, can they clean the rest of the house, too?" I joked.

"You need a demolition crew for that," Mickey said, looking around. "You said that you brought the money to him yesterday. Was it a check? I know Crenshaw hated banks, so it would be strange for him to take a check."

"Yep, I had to bring him money in cash. 250K to be exact."

"Damn, robbery should never be a good reason for murder. Do you know what he did with the money?"

"I have no idea. I gave him the gym bag with the money, he took it in the house, then came out with my empty bag. I was outside so I didn't see what he did with it."

"Well, I'll have to say this is a robbery. Do you have an idea where he might have put it?"

"His office is over here, you can check there. Or would you like to go look under his mattress," I said with a grin.

"No, smartass, we can start with the office." I led them to the door, which was already open. The Crime Scene people were standing in the middle of the room.

One man turned to us and said, "Anyone know if this place was tossed or was Crenshaw just a slob?"

"I was in here yesterday with him, this is how it looked." I saw a wall safe but it wasn't opened. I went to it and tried the handle, it didn't budge. "I'll have to get a locksmith out to open this."

"When you do let me know if the money is in there. It doesn't look like they searched very hard, this all looks like an organized mess." Mickey said. He turned to the CSU leader and asked, "Are you about done?"

"We've dusted everything someone could have touched, and found nothing else. So I'd say we were finished. It's all yours." He called to his team and they left.

"Well, Jake, I hope you are happy with your cemetery. There have been a number of ghost sightings in the cemetery over the last few years, so don't get spooked." He laughed and went out of the room.

I looked at Scott and said, "He's still a jerk."

Scott agreed, "I only tolerate him when we are at a scene."

We left the room and about a half hour later, the place was cleared of cops and their cars. I stood looking at the blood and decided I didn't want it there. I went into the kitchen and found a pantry, but there was very little in there to clean with. I went back to the room with the furnace and found some buckets and mops. On a shelf was some bleach, which I knew would clean blood.

I filled one bucket half full of water and poured in most of the bleach. I took a mop and went out to the blood. I spent about twenty minutes wiping the area and got most of it out. It at least looked better. I took everything back to the furnace room and then went out the front door to the road. I stood staring at the cemetery and wondered what I was going to do now.

I heard a phone ring in the house, so I went to answer it. "Hello."

"Who am I speaking to?" came a female voice.

"Jake Wyler, the new owner of the cemetery. May I help you?"

"I was told by my assistant that Ben Crenshaw was murdered."

"He was, the police just left here. Now I have to figure out how to run this place since Ben was supposed to explain it all to me. And you are?"

"Tracey Fuller, director of the Fuller Funeral home. I was trying to get hold of Ben to have a body buried next to his wife."

"Yes, I heard about it. Give me a name and if you have any information as to where his wife is buried, I'll try and find her. I'll need to get a hole started and then you can bring the man here. I have to say, I'm new at this so be patient with me."

"I understand, I'll send you the information on my client. Do you have an email address?"

"Yes," I said and gave it to her. My laptop was at home, so I'd have to bring it in to use it. I had noticed a computer on Crenshaw's desk, I'd have to see if it worked. I couldn't see him on a computer.

We finished the call and I went back out to the road. A car was just driving in and I could see Becky at the wheel. She pulled up to me and got out. Paul was with here and he came over to us.

"Jake, I heard about Crenshaw. What happened?"

"Don't really know. The detective thinks it may be a robbery, because of all the money I gave Crenshaw. But how could anyone know about that? Only you and a few people at the bank knew. Plus a couple people at the library I was working at. But I know all these people and they wouldn't murder him for the money."

"For that much money, anyone could have done it."

"Even you?" I said with a smile.
"Thank you so much," she huffed.

Chapter 9

"Take it easy, I was kidding. I'm sure you'd never murder someone. How did you hear about Crenshaw?"

"This is a small town, or did you forget? The guy from the funeral home just had to make a big deal out of it. One of the women at the bank told me. I'm on my lunch hour and brought Paul over to talk to you. I'm sorry about Crenshaw, but it shouldn't stop your routine here."

"You should be a motivational speaker. If you have to leave to go back to work, I can take Paul home."

"I was hoping you'd say that. I'll let you two work out the job requirements. I have to go. Thanks, Jake." She turned and went to her car and drove out as we watched.

"She's a determined woman," I said.

"I sometimes have to hold her down or she'll try saving the town."

"So, let me show you what I need done." I took him to the shed and opened it. We pulled out the lawnmower and Paul started it up. It surprised me that he got it working so fast. I could see he was going to be an asset.

"You need the grass cut, I'll start on the front."

"Don't we need to talk about pay?"

"I'm sure you'll be fair, my mom likes you, so I trust you." He took the mower and moved over to the cemetery. I watched him zipping the mower around cutting the grass around the headstones.

I had a mystery to solve. If the killer or killers didn't find the money, that means it's still in the house. I needed to call a locksmith and get the safe opened. I went to the office and used the desk phone to call the locksmith after looking for one in the area with my cell phone. I arranged for someone to come out this afternoon and hung up.

I went to the computer Ben had on his desk and started it up. It was old and still had Windows 95 on it. I could upgrade the operating system to bring it into the twenty-first century.

Now to search. I opened the desk drawers and pulled them out. I looked underneath each one, looking for anything he may have taped under them, a note or a key. There was nothing to be found, so he wasn't that clever. I looked around the room and all I saw were walls that had wainscoting halfway up. There were posts every ten feet and I went to knock on the walls. They all sounded solid.

I looked over to the safe and figured he put the money in there. I would just have to wait. I could hear the lawnmower chugging away outside and was glad for Paul's help. I opened my cell phone to the mail program I had installed. I never got many emails, mostly spam and ads.

I found the email from the funeral home and opened it. The name of the deceased was Dan Howey and his departed wife was Mary. I saw a book on the desk with entries listed and ran through them until I found Mary Howey. The notation showed that she was in lot four, row ten. I saw a map on the wall that showed the layout of the cemetery and found the area detailed as lot four. I had to get my head into the direction of the map and figured out where she would be.

I left the office and went out to the area I figured was lot four. I walked down the row of headstones until I found Mary. I was pleased with myself and saw the empty space next to her for Dan. Now, I had to get someone to dig the grave. I went back to the office and looked for some type of phone book that he may have kept. I found it in one drawer and thumbed through it until I found Berney Excavating. I figure it had to be the people who would dig the holes.

I called the number and explained who I was. "You need a hole dug?" the voice on the phone said.

"Yes, and I'm the new owner of the cemetery. Now I need a hole dug for a body, did you do this for Crenshaw?"

"Yes, we did. I can have the equipment and a man out this afternoon, if that's good for you?"

"Please, I'm new to this and any help is good for me. I'll be here."

"Where's Crenshaw?" he asked. I guess the news hadn't gotten to him yet.

"I don't know if he was a friend of yours, he was murdered last night."

"Wow, that's too bad. He was an ornery man but I liked him. I'll have the man out this afternoon."

I thanked him and said good-bye. I hung up and felt good that the day was going well. Grass was being cut, the body was scheduled to be buried and the hole was going to be dug. Oh, and the safe would be opened, solving one mystery.

I didn't hear the lawnmower running so I went out and found Paul walking back to me.

"I'm out of gas, there's none in the shed. I found this empty can and I'll need to get some more," he said.

I looked over to my car. It was a ten year old Chevy and I wasn't so concerned about it getting wrecked, so I gave him the keys. "Go to the Speedway down the street and get some. I dug out Twenty dollars and gave it to him. He smiled and said he'd be careful with my car. I wasn't worried about it, I just didn't want him getting in an accident to hurt himself, but I figured he was a cautious driver. He drove off and I stood looking at the porch. Now I would need a carpenter to fix it.

Paul came back with the gas and gave me the change. I asked him if he was good at carpentry.

"I did some in woodshop class. We built a small house to sell for new equipment for our woodworking shop we needed due to budget cuts. I know how to handle a hammer. I suppose you want this porch fixed." He said with a grin.

I had to admit the boy was smart.

Chapter 10

Paul went back to cutting the lawn, as I waited for the locksmith and the hole digger. I went back into the office and started to rummage through the mess Crenshaw left. I got a garbage bag from the kitchen and threw out a ton of things I knew wouldn't pertain to me. I finally could see the top of the desk. I sat and organized everything, then sat back to relax.

I heard a loud noise outside that sounded like a big truck and looked out the dirty window. It was the excavating people. I went out to greet them.

"Mr. Wyler?" A youngish man asked me.

"I am. I'll show you where to dig the hole." I led him over to the plot and he said he'd get on it.

"Did you do a lot of hole digging for Crenshaw?" I asked as we walked back to the truck.

"Sure, a couple times a month. This place isn't as busy as the four other cemeteries in the county, but he had his share."

I moved away as he drove the truck down the road to the plot. I didn't really want to see the hole being dug so I started back to the office. I was on the porch when I saw a pickup truck driving in. It was the locksmith. Everything was falling into place.

The truck parked in front of the building and an older man got out. He came to me on the porch. He looked down and said, "This porch needs fixing."

"Yes, I'm working on it. Now, I need a safe opened, can you do that?"

"Short of using nitro glycerin, I can open just about any safe. Take me to it."

I took him into the office and pointed to the safe.

"Wow, that's an old safe. Has to be about forty years old, but I can open it. It's a Crestwell safe. They went out of business twenty years ago, but I still see a number of them around. Let me get my tools," he said and left the room.

I looked out the window and saw Paul about half way down the area. I figured he'd need a break and it was almost dinner time for me. I went out and yelled for him. He was close enough to hear me and shut off the mower. I waved him to come over.

"Yes, sir," he said.

"Call me Jake, if we are going to be working together. Now I'd like you to drive over to the Subway and get us a couple subs. I want a twelve inch club, with ranch dressing, and get whatever you want." I dug out another twenty and handed it to him along with the keys. He grinned and went off. I followed the locksmith back in the house and to the room. He dropped his bag and studied the safe.

"I presume you don't have the combination?"

"If I did, I wouldn't need you," I said with a grin.

"Some of these old safes are temperamental, so even if you have the combination, they refuse to open."

"I see. Well, I don't have it, sorry."

"No problem, give me a little time." He opened his bag and took out some kind of box and attached it to the safe. He plugged in earphones to the box and started to spin the dial. "Keep quiet," he said and listened.

I watched him spin the dial back and forth slowly, writing something on a note pad, then he took the earphones out of his ears and removed the box. He grabbed the handle and twisted it. The door opened and I moved closer, hoping my money would in there. I was disappointed. There were papers in the safe but no cash. Damn.

He stood back, smiling, "I knew I could open it."

"Make up your bill and I'll pay you," I said, getting my check book out of my back pocket.

He scribbled on a pad and tore off the top sheet and handed it to me. I looked at it and it wasn't too bad. I wrote a check and handed it to him.

"Pleasure doing business with you." He handed me a small sheet of note paper.

"Here's the combination, in case you still want to use this antique. I'd advise getting a new one. Thanks," he said and picked up his bag and left.

I looked into the safe and took out the papers. Most were just old letters from some woman named Agatha. They were love letters, which surprised me. I found one paper that had a diagram of plots and two had X's on them. They reminded me of a pirate's map, then it struck me. What if Crenshaw had buried money in these plots?

I went to the wall map and looked for the corresponding plots and I found they were labeled 'taken' but no name on them. Now this intrigued me. I had a feeling that Crenshaw was eccentric, Becky said he was crazy, but maybe he wasn't as crazy as he led people to believe. I went out to the cemetery and down the rows to the plots that Crenshaw had marked as taken. I was shocked to see two headstones, one marked "Benjamin Crenshaw" and the one next to it marked "Agatha Crenshaw". Now I was really confused. I had to read the letters to see what Agatha had to do with Ben.

I saw Paul drive back in and went to him. He handed me the bag of subs and I told him to follow me. I took him into the office and we sat. I opened my sub and ate as I told him about what I found in the safe and the graves.

"So Crenshaw had his grave ready for when he died?" Paul asked.

"I guess so, but who is the woman named Agatha? I have to read the letters from her to see how deeply he was involved with her."

"Maybe he murdered her and she's buried out there," Paul said with a sardonic grin.

Chapter 11

I had to laugh, "I certainly hope not. Although, it's been said that the place is haunted, so maybe it is Agatha who's doing the haunting."

Paul grinned and ate more of his sub. "So are you going to see if you can find the money you gave the old man?" he asked.

"I plan on it. Maybe after you're finished with the lawn you can come in and help me. I'll give you a finder's fee."

He started eating a little faster now. "I'd be happy to help," he said with a mouth full of sub.

"Don't choke on your food, the money isn't going anywhere. As long as the house doesn't burn down," I said jokingly, but then I thought that wasn't a good thing to say.

We finished up our subs, just as the man with the hole digger came in the office.

"I'm done, sir," he said politely.

"Boy, I hate to ask, but I have another hole to dig. Can you stay?"

"Sure, show me where and I'll get started."

Paul and I led him out to the plot and he read the headstone. "Wow, I guess old man Crenshaw had a feeling he'd need a plot. Who's Agatha?"

"I don't know yet, but I may have you carefully dig up the grave. Just to see if she's in there," I said.

"I've had to dig up a few coffins, so I know how to be careful. I'll call you when I'm ready."

I thanked him and Paul said he was going back to cutting grass. He went off and I went back to the house. I wanted to read the mysterious letters from the woman who carried Ben's name.

I sat at the desk and untied the ribbon around the letters, spreading them out by date on the letterhead. I started to read the first letter, "Dearest Benjamin, I had to write you to say I'm going to leave Harold. I have wanted to be with you for so long, I had to let you know. May we spend time together, even if it's just moments a week? Harold is so possessive that I'm afraid to get away from him. Please be patient with me, I'll see you soon," I read the ending as it said "Yours, Aggie"

"Wow," I said out loud. I couldn't picture Ben being a home wrecker. This Aggie must have seen something in the crabby old man I had met. I picked up the next letter and read that one, then the next. I felt strange reading such personal letters written long ago. The date on one letter said it was written in 1949, the year I was born. I wasn't sure exactly how old Ben was but he had to have been in his twenties, same as my parents when I was born. I read the last letter from the pile and this one was a warning.

"Benjamin, watch out for Harold, he suspects something and accused me of cheating on him with you. I denied it but he said he'd deal with you. Please be careful, I don't know what he may do. Love, Aggie."

Hmm...now the plot thickens. Did Harold go to Ben and was there a fight or possibly Harold was murdered by Ben and then he was free to marry Aggie? I hoped that her grave being dug up would solve this.

I stood and looked out the window. I could see the man digging up the hole for Ben, then he got off the scoop and looked down in the hole. I presumed he was seeing if he was deep enough, six feet down. He got back on the machine and dug some more.

I saw Paul pushing the lawn mower back to the shed, so I went out to him. "Finished already?" I asked.

"I trimmed around all the headstones and monuments, but the back area that has no graves is too overgrown for the lawnmower. Crenshaw never bothered to have it cut."

"I'll have a lawn service come in to cut it down. I'll see about getting a riding lawnmower so it will be easier for you."

"Sounds great. Now, shall we go see how Crenshaw's grave is doing?"

He sounded as anxious as I was, so we walked over to the gravesite and watched the man work. He waved and then checked the hole again. He got back on the machine and moved it over to the grave of our mysterious Aggie.

He carefully dug until he was about three feet down when he hit something. He stopped and got off his machine, going to the hole. Paul and I went there and saw a metal box that had been dislodged by the shovel. The man stepped down and grabbed a handle on the box and yanked it up. He tossed it up to the ground and I bent down to examine it. It looked as though it had been in the ground for years and there was a padlock on the hasp.

"Do you want me to keep digging?" he asked.

"Yeah, just until you see if there's a coffin in there." I was anxious to open the box but I wanted to know if Aggie was actually buried here. The man dug further and then said, "That's as deep as a grave should go. Nothing in there."

I was disappointed but glad we didn't find a body. I told him to fill it in and see me about the bill. I pulled up the box and Paul followed me to the house. It wasn't heavy, about two feet long and one foot wide. It looked like a safety deposit box. I took it into the office and set it on the floor to clean it off. I led Paul to the back room where we got some rags and in a corner were some tools on a table. I found a hacksaw and brought everything back to the office. Paul took the rags and started to wipe the box down as I tried to saw the old lock off the hasp.

We both finished and the lock was now off. I opened the box and looked in it. I made a gasp.

Chapter 12

I reached into the box and took out a plastic bag filled with money. That felt great, but under the bag were a gun and some papers. I handed the money to Paul, "Put this on the desk," I said.

I reached in and carefully lifted the gun by the butt end. It was an Army .45 and it was slightly rusted but in good shape. I didn't know if Ben had been in the military, but then remembered he said he drank with my old man at the VFW. So he was in the military. I set the gun on the desk and pulled out the papers. They were clippings from different newspapers about the murder of a local man named Harold Turner. The police had no leads and suspected his wife, but couldn't prove it. In those days there was no forensics to prove much. I wondered if this gun killed Harold and if it was Ben or Aggie who shot him.

Paul read as I handed him each clipping and then I went to the desk, picking up the gun with a tissue from the box on the desk. I didn't know if fingerprints would still be there after sixty years.

"Shouldn't you call the police or something?" Paul asked.

"Only if we don't mention the money. They'd want to take it as evidence. I'll call later, this is a sixty year old murder, and everyone is dead, so it doesn't matter how much longer I stall."

Paul looked at the gun and said, "Does it even matter if you call them or don't call them. As you said, everyone is dead so who are they going to arrest?"

He was right, why sully Ben's memory if the crime is moot now. I took the gun, clippings and money and put them in the safe and closed the door. I just hoped I could reopen the safe.

There was a knock at the office door, it was the man from the excavating company. I told him to come in and I'd write him a check. He looked at the box on the floor.

"What did you find in it?" he asked.

I didn't want to say what was actually in the box and I saw the letters on my desk, so I lied. "It had love letters from Agatha to Crenshaw. I guess he wanted to save them in her empty grave."

"I don't suppose you know where she ended up?" he asked.

"I have no idea, but I'm going to investigate. How much do I owe you?"

He handed me a bill and I wrote another check. I could see this was going to deplete my checkbook. I tore it out and handed it to him.

"I'll see about starting you an account for future digs," he said and thanked me. He went out as Paul and I watched him go.

"Quick thinking," Paul grinned.

"I hate lying to people, but it wasn't any of his business."

"Who did you lie to?" came a voice from the doorway. Paul and I both jumped as Detective Mickey France stepped in the room.

"I don't have to share information with everyone. I had to tell the guy what we found in a grave."

"What did you find in a grave?" he asked pointedly.

I lied again, and to a cop. "A box with love letters from a woman to Crenshaw. It was buried in a grave next to where Crenshaw had his grave prepared."

"Is that why David was here to dig a grave?"

"Yes, Fuller Funeral home had me get a grave ready for their body. Plus we found that Crenshaw has a gravesite waiting for him, so the guy dug it up also. When can I bury him?"

"It's still an ongoing investigation and his body is still with the ME. Now, where were you the night Crenshaw was murdered?"

"I don't like the insinuation, but I was on a date with this young man's mother from seven until midnight."

He looked at Paul and said, "Can Becky confirm that?"

"I can confirm that. She was with Jake out to dinner, then I don't want to know what else they did. He brought her home by midnight."

I was trying not to laugh about his comment as to what his mother and I did after dinner. I'm sure he figured it out.

"Okay, you're covered, Jake. Now, have you found the money yet?"

"It's been a busy day and I haven't had time to look. But I'll keep you informed as to where my money is."

"Your money?" he said, cocking his eye.

"Yes, it was my money to begin with and since he's dead and I'm owner of his property and whatever is in the house, it's still my money. I hope you don't have a problem with that," I said firmly. "Shouldn't you be out rounding up suspects?"

"I had hoped I would be able to take you in for questioning, but I guess that's no longer needed. I'll need a list of anyone that you knew of who had information about the money you gave him." I said I'd have one for him later.

He looked down at the box. "So Crenshaw buried love letters in this box?"

"I held up a few of the letters and said, "Yep, he was sentimental, I guess. Burying his lost love."

"I knew he was crazy, but I'd just burn old love letters, not bury them. Okay, I'll be in touch." Then he said to Paul, "Tell your mom I said hi." He went out and I followed him to lock the front door to keep any more intruders out. I went back to the office and sat at my desk. Paul said, "France is a jerk." I agreed.

Paul sat reading the letters. "I feel sorry for Crenshaw," he said. "It must have been hard to love a married woman."

"I just hope they didn't murder her husband. I think I may need to follow up and see if I can find out what happened to Aggie after the murder of her husband. Crenshaw had the headstone printed with his last name on her grave. They must have married eventually. I feel like a little detective work."

"I'd like to help," Paul said.

"We'll start tomorrow," I replied.

Chapter 13

"I better get you home or your mother will hold me responsible for corrupting you," I said and took Paul out to my car.

As I drove him, I said, "I appreciate your wanting to help me. I have no idea what I'm doing and it helps to have someone as a buffer. We can go on a search tomorrow to find out what happened to Agatha, then back to hunt for Crenshaw's hiding place with my money."

"Hey, this is more exciting than anything else I've done this year. I'm happy to help you," he said. "Do you really feel the money is yours?"

I thought on that. "Good question. Crenshaw hid the money in the house and it's mine now. He died leaving no relatives, so I have to claim it as mine. I'm sure it's weak, but the cops will try and nab the cash as evidence, I'm just protecting my interests."

"Finders, keepers," Paul said.

"Right!" I replied.

I arrived at his house and said, "It was great having you help today. I'd be a nervous wreck with everything that happened."

"Well, I enjoyed it. I don't even mind the hard work. I'll come by tomorrow around nine, if that is all right?"

"Sounds good. I have to go Walmart and get a few things before I stay my first night in the haunted house," I joked.

"Okay, then, see you in the morning," he said and got out. I waited until he was in the house and then saw Becky at the door. She came out to the car and I rolled down the window.

"So, did you two bond?" she asked, leaning in.

"You have a great son, I wouldn't mind having a couple of him as sons. It was a crazy day and it's going to get crazier. I'll tell you all about it on our next date."

"Oh, so you decided that we are having another date. Maybe I don't want one."

I stared at her until she broke out laughing. "Don't worry, stud, your date book is full." She laughed again and went back to her house. I watched her walk, it was a nice walk. She had a movement that I enjoyed.

I drove to the all night Walmart and bought one of those inflatable beds with the built-in pump, and a pop-up lantern. I drove back to the house and parked in the front. I noticed a light on in the window of the office and I didn't remember leaving it on.

I reached under my seat to where I kept a tire iron for protection against carjackers. I got out and went to the door, it was slightly open and I carefully pushed it in. I stood just inside listening, and heard a slight rustling from the office.

"I'm coming in and I have a weapon!" I yelled, and then thought about Crenshaw being shot. I stepped back outside but still looking at the office door.

The light went out and I saw a dark figure run out and to the back of the house. I waited, until I heard a door open and close. I knew I had an old handgun that was my father's from the war. He kept it clean and in working order. I went back down off the porch and to the car. I drove to my apartment and went in to get the gun from my closet. I had kept it for home protection, but it was never loaded. I could never decide if it was better loaded or unloaded. I grabbed the box of ammo and went back out to the car.

I was now nervous about the break-in. That meant the killer hadn't found the money, so it must still be in the house. It was now almost midnight and I was tired, but I knew I couldn't sleep. I took the bed and lantern into the office, closed the door and rammed a chair under the knob. I hoped that would keep anyone out, so they couldn't break in. I turned on the light, and looked around the room. There were only two windows, one on the front and one on the side. I knew they were painted shut since I already tried to open them earlier to air out the room.

I didn't figure the robber would come in through the window since he seemed able to open the front door. I'd have the locksmith come back out to install a deadbolt. I was surprised that Crenshaw didn't have the house locked up better.

I took the mattress out of the box and plugged the pump in, turning it on. The thing inflated quickly and then I shut it off. I realized I had no sheets but didn't want to go upstairs to get some. I had the gun now and I loaded it, feeling a little safer. I found a small blanket on a chair by the window. Now I had covering for the night.

I set the lantern and gun next to the bed and stretched out, covering myself with the blanket. It had an odd smell, like an old person's smell, Vicks maybe. I had left the room light on and closed my eyes, but I knew they would open often to check the room.

I must have fallen asleep, I was really tired and now the sun was coming in the side window. I looked at my watch, it was just after eight and Paul said he'd be here at nine. I got up, still in my clothes and took the chair from the door. I picked up the gun and opened the door slowly standing from the side. There were no shots through the door and it was quiet in the foyer. I looked out and saw no one. The front door was still closed so I came out.

I carefully went and opened the front door and was startled by Becky standing there. She saw the gun in my hand and said, "Don't shoot, I'm a friend."

Chapter 14

"Sorry, I was being cautious," I said and tucked the gun behind my belt. "Please, come in,"

"I just wanted to drop off Paul. I have to be at the bank by eight-thirty to open by nine. You can explain the gun later," she said with a smile.

Paul came up the porch looking grumpy. "Morning," he barely said to me.

"Good morning to you. I have a lot to tell you, come in and go to the office."

He went off and I moved to Becky giving her a big kiss. "Well, that was a nice way to start my day," she grinned.

"I have more if you want them," I grinned back.

"We can talk about that later," she waved her hand and went off the porch to her car. I closed the door and locked it. Back in the office Paul was in a chair, waiting.

"Someone broke in last night, while I took you home and went to the store."

His eyes widened and said, "Did they find the money?"

"No, I interrupted them, nothing looked changed in here. So I guess they didn't find anything. But I'm worried they will be back." I took the gun from my belt and set it on the desk.

His eyes went wide again, "Is that loaded?"

"Yes, it is. An empty gun doesn't do much, does it?"

"I wouldn't think so. Are we still going to look for Agatha?"

"I plan on it. Now where do we start?"

"What year was her husband murdered?" Paul asked.

"The newspaper said it was 1950, June 12th. I supposed we could go to the county building and go through their list of births and deaths. The register usually contains info about the persons and why they died. We can at least track any relatives and go from there."

"I'm ready when you are," Paul said, looking anxious.

I smiled at his exuberance and stood. "Let's go."

We went to my car and drove to the county building.

On the way I asked, "Does your mother date much? I know it's not my business, but I was curious."

He laughed and said, "She's gone on two dates in the last year. She hated both times, said the men were trying too hard to be macho. You were the only one she actually liked."

I liked that comment. Not that I wanted a relationship, but it was nice to have a female friend I can take on dates and whatever afterwards. "Well, since I've been back here, I haven't dated any woman, of course, I've only been back for about four months. When I was living in D.C. I never went out with the city women. They only wanted rich politicians, I was just a lowly clerk."

"How did you last all these years never being married?"

"I just wasn't interested. I saw from my parents what a marriage could do and decided it wasn't for me. My father was very abusive to my mother and me. I'm sorry to say, but I hated the man. I didn't even come back from D.C. when he was buried. He's in my cemetery, as a matter of fact. I just hope he doesn't haunt me."

Paul laughed and said, "I never met my birth father, he ran out on my mother after I was born. I guess I can say we both hated our fathers." He went silent.

"I knew your father, he was in our high school and he wasn't someone you could like. I was surprised when your mother said he was your father. I couldn't see her with him. You're better off without him."

"Is he still around?"

"I don't know, I haven't been here long enough to know what's what. Are you curious to know?"

"I'd like to tell him what a bastard he was for leaving my mother high and dry. She suffered on welfare and trying to hold any part-time job she could find while raising me. Babysitters took most of her pay."

"Well, give it time, he may show up one day for you to tell him off."

I pulled into the county building parking lot and we got out. We had to go through a metal detector checkpoint and then I asked where the register of births and deaths were. The officer told me and we went there.

There wasn't a very long line, thankfully. I got to the counter and asked the girl, "I need to see a list of deaths in 1950." She pointed to a row of computers and said, "Go there, it will provide you with that information." I wish I had known that before standing in line.

We went to an open cubicle and sat. I hit the enter key and the screen lit up. It asked for me to enter a year. I typed in 1950 and then a spreadsheet of names appeared. Paul was watching over my shoulder as I scanned down the names.

I got to June of that year and slowed the image. Paul saw it first, Harold Turner. We read the listing and found it said reason for death, murdered. There was a next of kin listing for a daughter, Kelly Turner and an address. I pulled out my note pad and wrote down the address.

"Okay, we have narrowed down the investigation. Shall we go visit Kelly?"

"If she's still there," Paul said, and I agreed.

We drove to Roseville and found the house. "I'm not sure how to handle this," I said as we sat watching the house. "I guess we just go to it." I got out, followed by Paul.

I knocked at the door since there was no doorbell. Shortly, a woman answered. "I'm not interested in religious materials, so go away." She started to close the door.

"Kelly Turner?" I blurted out. She stopped closing the door and opened it back up.

"I'm not Turner any more, I'm a Williams now. Why are you looking for Kelly Turner?" she asked.

Chapter 15

"Was your mother Agatha Turner?" I asked.

She didn't say anything at first. I was afraid she'd close the door, but she finally said, "Yes, what's it to you?"

"We were acquaintances of Ben Crenshaw and he knew her."

"Don't mention that man's name to me. He ruined my mother's marriage and I'm sure he murdered my father."

"So, you knew what happened? May we talk?"

She hesitated. "You still haven't told me why you're looking for my mother."

"I came into possession of letters your mother wrote to Crenshaw and I wanted to return them to her."

"I'm sure that would really upset her, and she's not in good condition for bad news."

"She's still alive?"

"She's in the Redeemer Nursing Home, and she's just holding on. After my father was murdered, she went crazy and it took years to get her back to somewhat normal. Crenshaw tried to find her, but I refused to let him know where she was. He kept saying he wanted to marry her. He had to be crazy himself. How do you know him?"

"Well, he owned a cemetery in Fraser and I just bought it from him. I found the letters he kept in a safe from your mother. Crenshaw was murdered the night before yesterday."

She didn't look surprised, just said, "Good, now he'll leave my mother alone."

"I'm sorry for your loss. My father was an abuser and it killed my mother, so I understand your feelings."

"No one can understand the anguish I went through, but I'm sorry for you. Now if you have nothing further to discuss, I have housework to do." She closed the door, leaving us standing there.

I turned to Paul, "Well, we know where she is and she never married Crenshaw. I guess he had her headstone made hoping they would wed. Sad story for him."

"Are we going to visit her?" Paul asked.

"I hate to bother her, but I'd like to know what happened to Harold. I think there's more to this. Let's take a ride."

We drove over to Redeemer Nursing Home and went in. There was a circular counter in the lobby with three women manning the station. There were people everywhere, some older seniors lounging in chairs and men and women wearing smocks going back and forth through doors and hallways.

I stood until one woman looked at me and said, "May I help you?"

"We'd like to see Agatha Turner, please." I said.

She looked at a list and said, "Room 10, down this hall, on the right."

"Thank you," I said and we went to the door. I looked in before going in. It was a two person room, with pull around curtains to give privacy. I wasn't sure which woman was Agatha, so I went in. The first bed had a sleeping woman in it but on the end of the bed was a tag saying Marion Haller. I went to the next bed and the tag said it was Agatha. Paul stood back as I went to her side. She was awake but not moving.

"Agatha?" I said quietly.

She turned her head to me. She looked so old I wondered if she had aged worse than her years.

Her lips moved but nothing came out. I leaned closer and said, "Agatha, I'm Jake Wyler. Can you talk?"

She was louder now, "I can, what do you want?"

"I hate to bring this up but do you remember the night your husband Harold confronted Ben Crenshaw?" I wasn't sure if he had, I hope it would stir something in her mind.

I could see tears coming from her eyes. "That was so long ago, I didn't mean for him to die."

"Who, Agatha? Harold? How did he die?"

She strained to speak, "He went to confront Ben and he had his gun with him," she recalled with great effort. "I took a taxi to the house where Ben lived in the cemetery and I came in as Harold was holding the gun on Ben. I went to Harold and tried to pull the gun away, we fought. Ben came around his desk, but before he could stop us, the gun went off. Harold fell as I held the gun." She choked a little and I reached to a table to get her water. I held it to her and she sipped from the straw. "Thank you. Are you the police?"

"No, I knew Ben and found your love letters to him. I also found the gun, but I hid it. What happened after he was shot?"

"Ben said he would take us to my home and I would call the police and say I found him when I got home. Ben made it look like a robbery and took his wallet and watch. Ben said to tell the police that I was with him that evening, he would be my alibi. It was all so wrong, but I was scared. I was badgered so much by the police that I just shut down, or so they tell me. They put me in a hospital where I was for so long. Now, I'm better and in this place. Do you know Ben?"

"I knew him briefly," I said.

"I'd like to see him. I've asked my daughter to bring him to me, but she refused. Kelly hated Ben. Can you bring him to me?"

I choked a little, I hated to tell her the news. "I'm sorry, but Ben passed away the day before yesterday."

She sobbed silently, then looked at me with tears in her eyes. "I really missed him. Did he die peacefully?"

I lied and said, "Yes, he did. But he never forgot you."

"Thank you for telling me. All this time I worried about him, now he's in a better place."

I didn't even want to bring up the burial plot and the rest of the story. I looked at Paul, who also looked a little teary. "Agatha, we have to go, but I'll be back with your love letters, if that's all right?"

She reached over and grabbed my arm, "Please do that, I have no mementos of those days. They will help me to remember better times."

"Okay, we have to go, I'll be back," I said and she released my arm. She closed her eyes and we left the room.

"Damn, that wasn't easy," I said as we went out the door to the car.

"Poor woman, she lost out on so many years," Paul said.

"Shows that you have to hold on to what you have, despite what others expect of you."

Chapter 16

We got in the car and I drove out. "Okay, we need to make an attack on the hidden money so I can stop people from breaking into the house. I should post a sign on the front saying the money was found and spent. That should discourage them."

Paul laughed and said, "Where shall we start?"

"Anywhere you want, but it has to be fairly close to the front door. Crenshaw wasn't in long enough to hide the money anywhere in the back of the house, or upstairs. I'll take the office and you can take the living room."

We arrived at the house and went in. "Okay, try and find any hidden panels or loose floor boards under rugs. Just don't punch any holes in the walls, if you can."

I left him in the foyer, he headed to the living room and I went in the office. I knew Ben hadn't put the money in the safe, so there had to be another place he would put it.

I checked all the walls for moveable panels. There was wainscoting halfway up the walls and they didn't move. I pushed on the square wall pillars that stood every ten feet or so. I pulled out a shelving unit and looked behind the thing. No opening behind it. I tapped on the wall and it sounded thick, not hollow.

I lifted carpeting and checked the condition of the floorboards. Nothing moved or lifted. I crawled under the desk to see if there was an opening with a door, found nothing. I looked up to the ceiling but there was no way he could have gotten up there, unless he had a ladder. I climbed on the desk and lifted the ceiling tile and looked into two beady eyes of a fairly small rat. I screamed and jumped down.

Paul came running back in and said, "What?"

I told him what I saw and he laughed. "Not a laughing matter. It was a huge rat," I lied again. I was getting good at it now. "Find anything?"

"Nope, there were no hidden places that I could find."

I went out to the foyer and looked around. The large stairway leading upstairs was enclosed on both sides. I remember that Harry Potter lived under stairs, so I checked to see if there was an opening. Paul was right behind me when I found a latch and pulled on it. A door opened and inside was dark, but we could see boxes.

"There's a pop-up lantern on my desk, go get it."

He came back with it and I lifted the top and the light cut through the dark. My heart jumped as I saw a number of boxes. I found a nail in the wall and hung the lantern. Paul and I pulled out the boxes as I was dreaming of tons of money that he had stashed away for years.

We stood looking at five containers the size of file boxes and I knelt down to the first one. I tore off the tape holding it closed and lifted the flaps. There was newspaper covering whatever was in the box. I pulled out the papers and saw what looked like Christmas ornaments and garland.

"Damn, I have a feeling this is going to be another bust," I said.

Paul tore the tape off the next box and found more ornaments. He worked his way through the rest and found they all contained ornaments for Christmas and Halloween.

"I can't picture Crenshaw as being the festive type to decorate the house."

Paul was pulling out a few of the ornaments and said, "We could start a new tradition and decorate. Halloween is coming up soon."

I had to laugh out of frustration and said "Okay, we will decorate and have a party for the neighborhood kids. Halloween in a cemetery should be a new tradition."

There was a knock at the door and I went to look out the side windows around the door, it was Becky. I opened the door and told her to come in. She saw Paul standing in the midst of boxes.

"Are you packing already?" she asked.

"No, come look. We found these boxes under the stairs. They're filled with decorations for Christmas and Halloween. I didn't think old man Crenshaw was the type to put up decorations."

"He wasn't," Becky said. "Three years ago these boxes were supposed to go to the children's hospital in Mt. Clemens. Crenshaw bought the decorations trying to be kind, but he was involved in a disagreement with the director of the hospital. Seems the director didn't want these things from a man who owned a cemetery. It was a petty thing, I think only because he didn't like Ben. So, Ben kept them all these years."

I looked at Paul and said, "Well, that clears up another of Ben's mysteries. This man was full of mysteries." I turned to Becky, "Is that director still at the hospital?"

"As a matter of fact, he stepped down after a couple nurses accused him of sexual advances. The hospital board didn't want a scandal, so he's gone."

"Good, now we can get these to the hospital where they belong," I said.

"I have a friend who's the head of child rehabilitation; I'll talk to her and see about getting the boxes there. I'm sure they'd love to decorate for the kids."

"Glad they can use them. Now, what are you doing here?"

"I thought I would take you and Paul for dinner, if you two aren't too busy. Then you can tell me all the things that have transpired in the last two days. And why you had a gun this morning."

I grinned and said that sounded good to me. Paul agreed, and we followed Becky out.

"I'll drive," I said.

"Don't trust my driving?" she said with a fake pout.

"No, I just want to thank you for the dinner, so you can relax and be chauffeured."

"Now that works for me. You're not such a bad person, Wyler," she laughed as we went to my car.

Chapter 17

We sat in the Burger King and I said, "Love the ambiance of the restaurant you selected."

"I'm sorry, but I'm not rich like some people. So we eat burgers."

"Are you referring to me? You aren't supposed to know how much money I have. That's personal."

"I'm sorry, but I'm your banker, so I got to know what you're worth," she said with a grin.

"You only want me for my money," I said with a laugh.

"Of course, do you think I'm stupid? What I don't understand, if you have so much money in your account, why do you act like you're poor, scrimping on things and buying at the dollar stores?"

"That's why I have money, I don't spend it frivolously. I hope to be able to use it for a good cause one day."

"Plus, you keep finding money at the house," Paul said quietly.

"What? You're finding Crenshaw's fortune. It's been rumored that he was hoarding cash. I'm surprised it took so long before someone did him in for his money."

"My money. But we couldn't find what he did with it. Since he's dead, we may never know. Unless we tear the house apart."

"So, why the gun?" she asked.

"Uh, well, someone broke into the house last night and I brought the gun from my apartment for protection."

"What? Are you in danger? Is Paul in danger?" she said in a panic.

"Take it easy. It was only one incident and the person fled when I confronted them. I don't know who it was but it looked like a woman in the darkness."

"A woman? She was after his money?" She asked.

"I guess so. It's the only reason anyone would want to be in the house. It's been years and Ben never reported a break-in," I said.

"You would have had to know Ben, he would have beat any intruder, before reporting it. He wasn't fond of police."

"I'm finding that out. But someone was in the house and money is the only factor. So we have to find it before I'm overrun with intruders."

"I can stay the night at the house and we can continue looking," Paul offered.

"Thank you, Paul. If your mother doesn't mind, that is."

"I don't know, is it going to be dangerous?" she asked.

"If they think we're in the house, they may not enter. So I think we should be safe."

"Okay, but if he gets hurt, I'm coming for you," she warned.

"Never fear, he'll be fine," I said.

"Good, now tell me all the details about your adventures the last couple days."

I gave her the brief rundown of what had happened from Crenshaw's death to this morning with Agatha.

"So Agatha was the love of his life?" Becky asked.

"Yes, and she never knew that he wanted to see her. The daughter refused to help him find her. It's a sad story. I may see if I can find some way of getting her buried next to Ben, when she passes. It may take a little conniving, but I think I can do it."

"That would be nice, since Ben already had the grave prepared for her. Of course, that's a little morbid."

"Whatever, they deserve to be next to each other," I said.

We ate our burgers and fries then went out to the car. Becky was bouncing around, looking attractive. I was smitten with her, but I had to be cautious, I didn't want her to get any ideas.

We arrived back at the house and Becky got out. "Paul, if you are staying the night, will you need clean clothes?"

"Mom, I can survive an extra day in the same clothes. Drop some clean ones off in the morning," Paul told her.

"I can do that. I hope you two find the money. I'd hate to see you lose it."

"If it's in the house, we'll find it. Only a matter of time and perseverance. Thanks for the dinner, see you in the morning. Be careful driving home."

She gave me a quick kiss and went to her car and drove off. It was a nice night out for October, not cold or warm, just right. I turned to the house and it didn't look like it was broken into. I didn't have the gun with me, I didn't have a carry permit. I thought about getting one.

We went to the house and I unlocked the front door. "How did the person get through the door last night?" Paul asked.

I stood looking at the door and thought about it. I closed the door and locked it back up. Then I took out a credit card from my wallet and slid it down the doorframe to the bolt that held the door closed. It was a trick I learned early in my life. I managed to get the bolt pushed back and the door opened. "Easy enough," I said to Paul.

"Wow, I'll have to remember that," he said.

"Only if you're going to be a professional thief. Otherwise, don't use it."

We went in and it was quiet. "Where will I sleep?" he asked.

I said, "Hold on." Then I went to the kitchen and opened the fridge. I closed it and said, "We need to take a run to the store."

We went back to my car and I drove to Walmart again. We bought another air mattress and I got a case of beer. I also got a couple sets of sheets and blankets for the mattresses. I paid and we drove back to the house.

I pulled into the drive and up to the house. I noticed a light was on again. This time in the living room. "Damn, they just don't give up." I grabbed the tire iron and I told Paul to stay back.

I went to the house and heard Paul right behind me. "I told you to stay back," I said quietly.

"I'm not staying out here by myself," he replied.

"Okay, stay close." I went to the door, it was opened again. "I really need to get a deadbolt on this door."

Chapter 18

I carefully pushed the door open and looked to the office. The light was out, which I hoped meant there was no one in there. I looked to the living room where the light was on. I couldn't understand why someone would be breaking in and turning on lights. I figured they were stupid.

I could hear banging around and decided to make a run for the office and to my gun. I handed the tire iron to Paul and said quietly, "Stay here, and I mean it."

I took a breath and made a dash for the office. I heard a gunshot and made a dive into the office. I heard the bullet hit a wall as I scrambled to the desk. I grabbed to where I left the gun, but it was gone. I kept my head down. I peeked over the desk now to see a figure silhouetted by the light of the living room, standing at the office door. A hand reached in and flipped the light switch.

The figure was in all black and had a ski mask on. A voice from behind the mask said, "Come out, Wyler, I have your gun." I was shocked that the voice was female.

"Come out now, Wyler, or I start shooting."

I stood and came to the side of the desk, with my hands up and waited.

"Where's the money? You must have found it by now. Give it to me or I'll start shooting parts of your body."

"I don't know where it is, I haven't found it yet," I said, shakily.

"Okay, say good bye to your legs." The figure raised the gun, just as I saw a figure behind the culprit. I heard a thud and the person fell forward to the ground, but managed to fire the gun. The bullet hit a file cabinet, missing me by inches.

I saw Paul standing over the body with the tire iron. "You okay?" he asked me.

"I am now, thank you so much." I went to the body on the floor and we turned it over. I grabbed the mask and pulled it off. I was shocked to see it was one of the women who worked in the bank.

Paul inhaled slightly and said, "It's Miss Denison, a teller at mom's bank."

"She knew I was getting the cash for Crenshaw and must have come and killed him for it. I'm sure she also knew he didn't keep his money in the bank, so the only assumption was he kept it here."

I pulled out my cell phone and dialed 911. "I need to speak to the detective on duty," I asked the person who answered.

"There's no one here right now, any particular detective you want to talk to?" she responded.

"Detective France, can you get hold of him and tell him Jake Wyler needs him. We caught the killer of Ben Crenshaw."

"I'll notify him immediately, sir. Stay on the line, please."

I could hear her calling Mickey on a desk phone, probably. She came back and said, "Detective France is en route."

I thanked her and hung up. "We need some rope to tie her up," I said.

"I saw some in one of the decoration boxes," he said and went out of the room. He came back a few moments later and we tied the hands and feet of the woman. I picked up my gun from the floor and put it on the desk.

I heard a siren coming up the road and the car turned into the cemetery. Mickey came charging up the porch, through the open front door and to the office.

"What's the deal," he said when he saw the woman on the floor.

"We caught her in the house looking for the money," I said. "She took a couple shots at me, but Paul hit her from the back with my tire iron."

France bent down and lifted the sweatshirt and found a gun tucked in her belt. He carefully took it out. "How did she shoot you with this gun still in her belt?"

"She used my gun, it was on my desk."

"This is probably the weapon that killed Crenshaw. I'll have it tested. I'm presuming this case is closed."

"I hope so, I don't need any more intruders in my house."

"Have you found the money yet?" he asked, as he pulled his cell phone.

I told him we searched but hadn't found it. He called for backup and then hung up. About a half hour later the woman was taken into custody and Mickey said, "You could have called earlier, I was getting ready for bed."

"Hey, I don't schedule break-ins. They just happen. Be happy we got her."

"I'll talk to you in the morning, I have to go spend the night interrogating and booking her. Thanks for the lack of sleep." He went out of the house and everyone was gone.

Paul turned to me and said, "He's still a jerk." I laughed.

I turned to the file cabinet and examined the bullet hole. I was happy that the gun worked after all these years and wanted the bullet as a souvenir. I went around to the front and was going to pull the lower drawer but it was locked.

"I never bothered with this cabinet. I never paid attention to it. Give me the tire iron." He handed it to me.

I rammed the pointed end into the drawer and yanked at the lock. It broke open and the drawer slid out. There was a few files laying in it and I lifted them to find the bullet. As I lifted it, I was shocked to find my money, still in bundles and banded.

I let out a yell and Paul came over to see what was going on. He yelled, too.

We took the money out of the cabinet and put it on the desk. "Amazing, we searched everywhere, but never thought to look in the file cabinet. I guess it was too obvious, not being a hidden cache. I'm happy now."

Chapter 19

"I guess we don't have to search anymore," Paul said.

"Thankfully, yes. I have to get this back into the bank, I don't want it in the house anymore. We can take it in the morning." We went out to the car and brought in the things we bought at the store. I set the beer on the desk, took out two and handed one to Paul.

"You're old enough, aren't you?" I asked.

"I won't be 21 until next year," he said and took the can.

I held up mine and said, "Here's to next year. We have to celebrate."

We toasted and sat looking at the money. Paul said, "Wow, you got a cemetery and didn't have to pay for it."

"I'm feeling kind of bad about that. Poor Crenshaw, he didn't even get to enjoy his retirement. I'll have to do something nice in his memory." I reached over and took a bundle of a thousand dollars and tossed it to Paul. He caught it and asked, "What's this for?"

"For saving my life. If that crazy woman had shot me, I'd have been a cripple like my old man. It was good that you stayed by the front door where she didn't see you."

Paul grinned and took a sip of his beer. "Don't sip it, guzzle it," I said and took a swig of my beer.

We sat just talking into the night, mostly about my experiences as a youth in this town. Paul told me that he and some friends were the ones who started the ghost stories about the cemetery.

"We would sneak in late at night and shine lights and howl. Crenshaw would come running out and stand watching for anything to move. We were already gone."

"That's funny, now let's get your bed set up." I stood and went to the new mattress and plugged it in to inflate it. We put the new sheets on and then called it a night.

The next morning we were up and getting ready for the day. I had a body to bury next to his wife, after calling the funeral home. They said they would be out in the afternoon, after the wake. I called the police station and got hold of Mickey.

"I need Crenshaw's body so I can bury him," I said.

"We turned him over to the Fuller Funeral Home for prep, you can talk to them about dumping him in the ground. Oh, and the woman confessed to killing Crenshaw, it seems she has a gambling addiction and borrowed heavily from a loan shark. She lost it all at Motor City Casino and she was worried about paying the loan back. She thought about embezzling from the bank, but then you showed up to get your money to take to Crenshaw. She waited until night time and went to rob him. Unfortunately, Crenshaw tried to stop her and the gun she brought went off, killing him. She never found the money, so the case is officially closed."

He didn't ask about the money and I wasn't going to offer. We finished and hung up. I had to get hold of the funeral home and see about burying Ben. I picked up the love letters from Agatha and tied them back up with the ribbon. I'd take them to her later, after the burial of the husband.

Paul came back in to the office. I had sent him to pick up a breakfast meal at Burger King. We sat eating when I heard the front door open and close. Becky came into the room.

"Good morning, sunshine, we caught the killer last night," I told her.

"What? You two caught the killer? Who was it?"

Paul grinned and I said, "Tell her."

He looked to his mother and said, "Miss Denison from the bank. She tried to shoot Jake, but I hit her in the head with a tire iron."

"What!!" she yelled. Then looked shocked and went to sit on a chair. "Denison? I can't believe that. You hit her in the head?"

"Yep, he's a hero, he saved my life," I said.

She looked to the money on the desk. "Oh, my god. You found the money?"

"Yes, it was in the most obvious place that we kept overlooking." I explained everything from coming back from the store until the police took Denison away and finding the money.

"I don't believe she would do something like that. It shows you never know people." Then she saw the empty beer cans. "Jake, I presume you drank all that beer?"

Paul and I both giggled.

"Honestly," she said to Paul. "I let you stay the night and you get involved in a crime and get drunk. We have to have a long talk."

"Talk to me, it's my fault," I said.

"I'll deal with you later. Now, are you putting the money back in the bank?"

"As soon as I get the gym bag out. You can get a deposit slip ready for me. Oh, and do I get a gift for the deposit?"

"No, you already got a toaster. Are you going to move into the house now?"

"I may as well, no sense having two places to live. I'll start after we bury Ben this week."

"I never knew him, but I feel sorry for him. He was quite a legend in this town. Well, I have to go to work. I brought you some clean clothes, Paul. They're by the front door." She stood and stuck her tongue out at me and went out.

About an hour later, the people from the funeral home came to set up the burial plot. I watched them from my window, now clean. Paul was cleaning all the windows in the house and washed down the fridge for the beer.

The funeral procession pulled into the property and they had a nice burial. Paul and I stood off the side to watch. The funeral director came to me and said, "We have Ben Crenshaw in, do you want to come in to select a coffin?"

"No, just pick one that's not expensive and send me the bill. Let me know when he can be buried."

She agreed and went off. "Let go take the love letters to Agatha," I said to Paul. We went and got them and drove to the nursing home. We knew where she was, so went to her room. She wasn't there. "Where is she?" I asked a woman changing the bed sheets.

"Sorry, she passed away last night. Monty Funeral Home took her."

That took me back. Now I felt really bad about the whole affair. Paul and I went to the car and sat.

Chapter 20

"Now what?" Paul asked. I started the car and drove to Monty Funeral Home. We went in and I asked for the director.

"May I help you?" a man asked.

"You have a woman named Agatha Turner, who was brought in last night?"

"We do, she's being prepped. Are you family?"

"No, have burial arrangements been made yet?"

"No, the daughter is still trying to deal with her mother's death."

"I want to pay for the entire funeral. As an anonymous donor, but the woman has to be buried in the Fraser Cemetery. Will that be a problem?"

"I'll let the daughter know. I'm sure we can come to an agreement. She doesn't have much money and Agatha had no insurance. Who are you?"

"Jake Wyler, I own the cemetery where I'd like her to be buried." I took out my note pad and wrote down my number, then handed it to him. "I need to get some cards made up," I said to Paul. "Call me when you make the arrangements and I'll have a plot ready."

"This is most generous, Mr. Wyler. I'll keep you informed. I'm sure the daughter will accept the offer."

"Thank you," I said and took Paul out to the car. "At least Ben's money will do some good for his old flame."

Two days later, we had Ben buried in a simple ceremony attended by Paul, Becky and four other people who had known Ben. The hole was closed by the same excavating company and I asked David to dig up Agatha's plot again. Paul and I moved the headstones so Kelly Turner wouldn't see the names on them.

The next day, Monty Funeral brought Agatha in and they had a burial ceremony. After it was over, Kelly saw me standing off the side and came over.

"You arranged all this, didn't you?" she asked. "Why, and what is your connection to my mother?"

"None. But I'd appreciate it if you'd read these," I said and handed her a manila envelope that I put the letters in. "If you don't want to keep them, just return them to me, please."

She didn't say anything, but turned and went back to her family.

"I hope she reads the letters," I said to Paul and Becky.

David filled in the hole, I told him to send me the bill and I took Paul and Becky to the porch.

"I wrote a check to the funeral home for the funeral, so it will come out of the money that was Ben's. I'm sure he'll be happy to be next to Agatha. Too bad they couldn't be together in life."

Becky kissed me on the cheek and said, "Good that we have each other in life."

"Shall we spend some of that time having a good dinner? No burgers."

I took them to the car and we drove out, leaving Ben, Agatha and all the other souls buried in the cemetery to their eternal peace.

THE END

Other Books by Bob Moats

The Jim Richards Murder Novels (in order) - Classmate Murders * Vegas Showgirl Murders * Dominatrix Murders * Mistress Murders * Bridezilla Murders * Magic Murders * Strip Club Murders * Made-for-TV Murders * Mystery Cruise Murders * Talk Show Murders * Sin City Murders * Black Widow Murders * Vegas Vigilante Murders * Area 51 Murders * Mortuary Murders * Hypnotic Murders * Sunshine State Murders * Blue Suede Murders * Honky Tonk Murders * Dark Carnival Murders * Lipstick Murders * Pasta Murders * Talent Show Murders * Shyster Murders * Campground Murders * Network Murders * Reunion Murders * Big Apple Murders * Kennel Murders * Trick or Treat Murders * Santa Murders * Wiseguy Murders * Toxic Murders * Private Eye Murders * Lonely Hearts Murders * Murder Vegas Style * Eulogy for Murder

READ about Jim Richards as a young man in the novella - Marriage Can Be Murder

* The Leviticus Murders - Detective Scott Murphy series book #1 * Last Call in Detroit - Detective Scott Murphy series book #2 * Seduction in Detroit - Detective Scott Murphy series book #3

* The Fatal Series - Fatal Rejection * Fatal Departure * Fatal Romance * Fatal Outbreak * Fatal Abduction * Fatal Seance

* The Doyle, P.I. series - Doyle's Law * Doyle's Justice * Doyle's Quest * Doyle's Paradise * Doyle's haunting

* The Gus Mackie novella series - Gus Mackie and the Hot Tamale * Gus Mackie and the Missing Princess * Gus Mackie and the Weeping Wife * Gus Mackie and the Lost Heiress * Gus Mackie and the Rock Star

* Stoney Hawk - female P.I.

* Also Bob's first juvenile book, "Crystal Prison of Kyr"

* My new paranormal ghost crime series - Ghost Squad 1 * Ghost Squad 2: Ghosts on the Loose * Ghost Squad 3: Mary Had a Little Ghost * Ghost Squad 4 - Haunted

Train Station * Ghost Squad 5 - Haunted Asylum * Ghost Squad 6 - Ghost Bride * Ghost Squad 7 - Death in the Family * Ghost Squad 9 – Dressed to Haunt

Now Available in Audiobooks: All 5 of the Doyle books, Three of the Gus Mackie books and nine of the Ghost Squad books. More Ghost Squad in the works. All books available on Audible, Amazon and iTunes.

Bob Moats Family of Readers

Thanks to the following people who are now part of the Bob Moats Family of Readers. They have read a book or more and enjoyed them. They all volunteered to be included in the list. If you are a fan of the books, send me your full name, and you will be included in future books. Send your name to books@bobmoats.com to be added here and on the website.

* ACHIM FEIFEL * AL Norris * Alex Wheatley * Alexandra Delporte-Wilkinson * Amy Morningstar * Andrea Bryan * Anne Shepherd * Arianda Sugar * Arlene Markowski * Ashley Augustus * Audra Hall * Barbara Hughes * Barbara Sammons * Barbara Schuler * Barbara Zirger * Beth Donohue Plenskofski * Beth Rosin * Betsy Childress * Beth Gibson * Betty Albrecht Vollmar * Bill Sandy * Bill Tornquist * Billie-jo Collie * Bob Lenski * Boni J Rychener * Candace Larson * Carl Bishopric * Carla Lewis * Carole Henderson * Carolyn Conroy * Carolyn Riddle-Linington * Cassy Bailey * Cathie Turner * Chad Hudson * Charlie Meier * Charlotte L Duran * Cheryl L. Everett * Cindy Ackley Nunn * Cindy Valstad * Connie Bancroft * Corinne Kay O'Daniel * Chris Krolczyk * Dana Robbins Chuchran * Dana Wichita * Daniel Kalus * Danielle Monique * Darren Heald * Dave Travers * David Wilkinson * David Wiman * Dawn Carpmail * DeAnn Jannereth * Deanna Miller * Deb Breuker Balbo * Deb Chenoweth * Debbie Carter * Debbie White * Deborah Fartuch * Deborah Gauze * Deborah Sullivan * Dee King * Denise Freeman * Devdatta Arun Gholkar * Diana Carver * Dianna Marie Juneau * Dianne Procopio * Dixie Beck * Donna Gould * Donna Thompson * Donny Minter * Doris Kight * Doris Shane * Eddie Moore * Edward Ringler * Eric Walters * Felicia Annette Bradfield * Fleur Wilkinson * Francine Menor * Gail Chesney * Georgiann Minster * George Conner * Greg Colucci * Hayley Rankin * Harold Garcia * Heidi Arnold * Herb Muir * Irma Ranee Coy * Jack Plunkitt * Jacqueline Moss * Jan Kimball * Janet Estep Lawson * Janice Schneider

* Janice Spoor * Jeanette Mulroy * Jennifer Besner * Jennifer Redmond * Jerry Dornak * Jessica Keown-Belous * Jim Beck * Jo Boguslaw * Joela Quaine * Jo Turner * Joanne Marie Turner * Joanna Wisniewski * John Gross * John Peiffer * John Wisbiski * Joseph Wauro * Joyce Stacy * Joyce Trifiletti * Judy Franklin * Judy Travers * Judy Padgett * Julie Heath * Junnahvee Benson * Karen Dahl * Karen Grams * Karen Higham * Karen Kaiser * Karen R. Merritt * Karen Meinburg Richwine * Karen Kirkman Parker * Karin Hawkins * Karin Vasvari * Karn Jones * Kathleen Donohue Roesing * Kathleen Riddle-Wolfe * Kathy Hinds Moore * Kathy Jones * Kathy Mitchell * Katie Benzler * Kay Burns * Kelly Cunko * Kelly Garcia * Ken Boggs * Keota Rodriguez * Kiera Mccarthy * Kim Estes * Kimberley May * Kitty Stolle * Kristie Sciler * Kirsty Stanton * LaLonnie Scallen * Larry Morris * Leann Parr * Lenora Scales * Leslie Marie Jackson * Linda Forester * Linda Bartley Florence * Linda Ingle Cox * Linda Kennerö * Linda Magill * Lisa Bower * Lisa Keller * Liz Gibson * Lorraine Wiman * Loretta Alexander * Lynda Bowles * Lynette Lawrance * LuAnn Louttit * Manny Rothman * Marc Berger * Marcia-Lee Finocchio * Marcia Gibson DeWitt * Marie Calder * Marlene Bryan * MaryLouise Kramp * Mary Lynn Gross * Megan Atkins * Meghan Hyden * Melissa Wescoat * Melody Cannavan * Meredith Simko Hanak * Michael Carruthers * Michael Dinkens * Michael Vannoy * Michelle Burns-Mitchell * Michelle Pilcher * Micki Potter * Mike Moats * Mikki Gregory * Mimi Baur * Merri Taylor * Myrna Hecht * Nadine Sutton * Nancy Ellen Sayre * Nancy Graveman Davis * Natalie Quine * Neena Martin * O'Della Wilson * Pamela Cooke Malone-O'brien * Pat Pollington * Pat Rohn * Patricia Jarmon * Patricia C Trezza * Patrick Barry * Paul Lawrance * Peggy Davis * Phyllis Bassett * Ray Zink * Raylene Matheny * Rebecca Collins Besner * Renee Brumley * Reta Hanna * Reta Moats * Robert Lenski * Roberta Meister * Roberta Navarro-Harder * Russ Holthaus * Sally Berneathy * Sally Hubler * Sandy Sillman * Sandy Schuman * Sara Swope * Sarah Santos * Satka Nikc * Sharon E. Edwards * Sharon Joiner * Sharon Mangini * Sharon McMillon * Sheena Rawl * Sherry Amstutz * Sherry Faller-Byrne * Sherry Tull * Shirley Alvarez * Shirley Davies * Shirley Williams * Stacie Rowe * Stephanie Conner * Steve Cullen * Sue Payne * Susan Haughton * Susan Hesse Adams * Susan Salomon * Suzan K Chase * Taisha Cullum * Tamara Moore * Tammy Castleberry * Tammy Lynn Wood * Ted Murphy * Terri Atkins * Terri Creech * Terry Raab * Theresa Miracle Harmon * Tonia Rachael Riggs-Williams * Tonya Mann * Travis Fleury-Lopez * Twyla Gawlas * Val Brooks * Walt Munsel * Willie Foust * Yvonne Isakson *

Thank you to all these wonderful people.

THANK YOU FOR PURCHASING this book. I hope you enjoy it as much as I enjoyed writing it for my faithful readers. Please feel free to email me to tell me what you thought about my stories. I love hearing from the readers. I can be reached at books@bobmoats.com

Thanks again!